FOG CAT

To the Dunham gang — Joel, Meghan, Amanda and Sarah — and to Katie Jolley, with love — M.H.

For Maureen Sparrow, who has never lost the heart of a child — P. M.

First U.S. edition 1999

Text copyright © 1998 by Marilyn Helmer
Illustrations copyright © 1998 by Paul Mombourquette

Kids Can Press acknowledges the financial support of the Ontario Arts Council, the Canada Council for the Arts and the Government of Canada, through the BPIDP, for our publishing activity. Canadä

Published in Canada by
Kids Can Press Ltd.
29 Birch Avenue
Toronto, ON M4V 1E2

Published in the U.S. by
Kids Can Press Ltd.
4500 Witmer Industrial Estates
Niagara Falls, NY 14305-1386

The artwork in this book was rendered in pen, ink and watercolor.
Text is set in Janson.

Edited by Debbie Rogosin
Designed by Marie Bartholomew
Printed in Hong Kong by Wing King Tong Company Limited

CM   98 0 9 8 7 6 5 4 3 2
CM PA   00 0 9 8 7 6 5 4 3 2 1

Canadian Cataloguing in Publication Data

Helmer, Marilyn
    Fog cat

ISBN 1-55074-460-7 (bound)   ISBN 1-55074-791-6 (pbk.)

I. Mombourquette, Paul.   II. Title.

PS8565.E4594F63 2000   jC813'.54   C97-932652-4
PZ7.H44Fo 1999

Kids Can Press is a Nelvana company

FOG CAT

WRITTEN BY

MARILYN HELMER

ILLUSTRATED BY

PAUL MOMBOURQUETTE

KIDS CAN PRESS

Hannah saw her for the first time the summer she came to live in Falls Harbor. The cat came out of the mist one gray August morning when Hannah and her grandfather were beachcombing. She stood on the rocks, a pale, thin wisp of a creature with eyes as green as the sea itself.

"Grandpa, look at the cat," Hannah called out.

At the sound of her voice, the cat vanished as quickly as she had appeared.

Grandpa looked after her. "That's the fog cat," he said. "Looks just like a wisp of fog, she does. She's been around these parts for a long time."

"Who does she belong to?" Hannah asked.

"She belongs to herself," Grandpa said. He picked up part of a lobster trap and tossed it toward a pile of driftwood.

Hannah looked at her grandfather. "Can we keep her?"

Grandpa shook his head. "You couldn't catch that cat any easier than you could catch a handful of fog, Hannah. She's gone wild."

Hannah looked at the spot where the cat had vanished like a ghost into the mist. "If I can tame her, can I keep her?"

Grandpa put his hand on Hannah's shoulder. "Maybe she doesn't want to be tamed."

"I could try," said Hannah.

Grandpa thought for a moment, then nodded. "You can try," he said.

"She needs a name," Hannah said. She looked out across the harbor. "I'm going to call her Fog Cat."

The next day, Hannah left herring scraps on a large, flat rock near the path to the cottage. When she and Grandpa came back from fishing, the scraps were still there, clinging to the rock like bits of dried seaweed.

"Maybe Fog Cat doesn't like herring," Grandpa suggested. "Some don't, you know." He winked at Hannah.

Hannah grinned. She didn't like herring very much either.

"I'll bet catching a cat is like catching fish." She looked up at Grandpa, shading her eyes from the sun. "You have to find the right bait."

That evening Hannah saved the lobster shells from supper. In the morning she scraped every last morsel from the shells. That afternoon the scraps were still on the rock, same as before.

Grandpa stared at the scraps. "Maybe she's not going to come," he said.

"She'll come," Hannah said. "When she's ready, she'll come."

When Grandpa wasn't looking, Hannah took a piece of finnan haddie from the fridge and put it out for Fog Cat. She walked back to the fishing dock to get her bait bucket, turning every few steps to look over her shoulder at the rock, until she lost sight of it. When she came back, the haddie was gone.

Hannah raced across the beach and tore up the steps to the cottage. She yanked the door open. "Grandpa, she came!" Hannah shouted. "Fog Cat came!" Her eyes were as round as sand dollars.

Grandpa turned from the stove, where he was frying onions. "Did you see her?" he asked.

"No, but the rock's clean." Hannah stopped to catch her breath. "She ate every last bit."

"Maybe it wasn't Fog Cat who took it," Grandpa teased. "Maybe the tide came in and washed the food away."

Hannah shook her head. "The tide hasn't come in yet," she said. "It was Fog Cat. I just know it was. And she likes finnan haddie, same as I do."

"Haddie?" Grandpa gave Hannah a long look. His lips twitched at the corners. "So that's where the haddie disappeared to. That was tonight's dinner."

"I just took my share," Hannah said. She opened the fridge. "I'll have scrambled eggs instead."

That night the fog crept across the bay on silent feet. In the morning it hung over the harbor like a soft gray blanket. It brought still, cool air and a cloudless sky. And it brought Fog Cat. She was at the rock when Hannah and Grandpa came along the beach that afternoon. She froze when she saw them and quickly vanished among the rocks as though the fog had swallowed her up.

Each day after that, Hannah moved the food closer to the cottage. She didn't see Fog Cat again, but when she and Grandpa came back from fishing, the food was always gone.

One morning Grandpa told Hannah that they wouldn't be going fishing for a few days. "The boat needs some work," he said. "Do you want to help?"

All morning Hannah worked on the boat, scraping and sanding. After lunch, Grandpa lay down for a nap. Hannah cleaned up the dishes and filled a plate with crab scraps. She put the plate on the ground and sat on the steps. She sat for a long time, until her bottom began to feel numb and her legs wanted to get up and run. Just when she thought she couldn't sit still for another minute, Fog Cat appeared.

Hannah held her breath. Fog Cat came closer, watching Hannah with her sea-green eyes. Hannah was surprised at her beauty. She was long and lean and silvery gray with dark ears and tail. There was a dark splotch under her nose, and her whiskers sprayed out like stiffly starched threads. Her eyes changed color in the sun and shadow, as the sea does.

Hannah watched her eat the scraps in quick hungry gulps. When she finished, she looked up at Hannah for a moment before she streaked away. From then on Fog Cat came every day, staying a little longer, venturing a little closer.

All too quickly, warm August breezes turned to cool September winds. Each afternoon Hannah burst into the cottage full of stories of friends and school. While Grandpa made hot chocolate, Hannah made up a plate of food for Fog Cat.

When she went out one afternoon, Fog Cat was waiting on the deck. Hannah was so surprised that she almost dropped the plate of tuna she was carrying. She knelt and held out the plate. Fog Cat came cautiously, nose twitching, ears alert.

The next day she let Hannah touch her. Her head was as soft as a down quilt. Her purr started up like the engine of Grandpa's old truck, rough and raspy until it had been running awhile.

One day a sleety snow fell from steel-gray skies and a chilly wind swept in from the sea. Hannah put a saucer of food inside the door and Fog Cat came into the cottage. When she finished eating, she explored from one end to the other. Finally she curled up on the hearth and went to sleep.

Winter stayed and so did Fog Cat. She came every afternoon, jumping onto Hannah's desk and marching boldly across her books while Hannah did her homework. Sometimes she brushed against Grandpa's legs, begging tasty tidbits when he cooked supper. In the evening she lay curled on the rag rug while the fire threw dancing shadows across her pale fur.

When Hannah and Grandpa went to bed, Fog Cat moved to the broad kitchen windowsill. There she spent the night. In the morning she waited by the door, pleading in her raspy, rusty voice to be set free again. Hannah didn't mind because Fog Cat always came back.

Winter passed and spring came with blustery days and waves pounding across the beach. As Hannah was finishing breakfast one morning, she heard the school bus rumbling up the road. Fog Cat was at the door waiting to go out, but when Hannah scraped the last forkful of egg into her dish, she came running. Hannah watched her.

"Grandpa, Fog Cat's getting fat," she said as she shrugged into her jacket and picked up her books.

Grandpa studied Fog Cat for a moment and turned to Hannah. "It's not the food," he said. "Fog Cat's going to be a mother." Hannah let out a whoop and threw her books in the air.

That evening Hannah began working on a special bed for Fog Cat. She cleaned out an old wicker basket and lined it with her baby blanket, which she kept tucked away in her bottom drawer.

One morning when Hannah got up, Fog Cat wasn't waiting at the door to go out. She wasn't on the windowsill or by the fire. Hannah tiptoed to the basket. She found Fog Cat curled in the folds of the blanket. Beside her were two tiny naked creatures. They looked like little pink mice.

Hannah knelt beside the basket. The kittens lay so still. Fog Cat looked up at Hannah and wailed, a sound as sad and lonely as the foghorn of a ship lost at sea.

Hannah scrambled to her feet. "Grandpa!" she shouted, pushing her voice over the tight lump in her throat. "Grandpa, come quick! Something's wrong!"

Grandpa came. He bent down and picked up the little bodies. They fitted easily into the palm of his hand.

"Are they dead?" Hannah asked.

Grandpa nodded. Tears stung Hannah's eyes. She felt Grandpa's hand on her shoulder. "We'll bury them," Grandpa said.

"On the beach," Hannah whispered, "where we saw Fog Cat the first time."

As Hannah reached over to stroke her, Fog Cat moved. Then they saw the third kitten. Hannah held her breath. The kitten moved and Hannah's breath whooshed out in a joyful gasp. "It's alive, Grandpa! Look, it's moving!" she cried. Fog Cat licked the kitten gently and nudged it closer. From then on, she stayed with it day and night.

One April day when the kitten was a month old, she set out on wobbly legs to explore the world beyond her basket. Grandpa watched her. "This little lady's going to make it," he said. "What do you plan to name her?"

"I don't know yet, Grandpa, but I'm thinking about it." Hannah rolled a marble toward the kitten. She had hardly dared to let herself think about a name. She had been so afraid that the kitten wouldn't live.

Suddenly Fog Cat was rubbing around Hannah's legs, asking in her rusty voice to go out. When Hannah opened the door, Fog Cat darted onto the deck. "Fog Cat …" Hannah called after her. The wind whipped the words from her lips. Fog Cat turned and looked back. Then she ran toward the beach and vanished among the rocks.

From that day on, it was Hannah who fed and took care of the little kitten, because that was the last time Hannah saw Fog Cat.

For weeks, she and Grandpa walked the beach, searching and calling. Every day Hannah put food out, waiting and watching the rocks where she last saw her. The food lay untouched. Fog Cat did not come back.

Sometimes still, on days when the fog hangs over the harbor like a soft gray blanket, Hannah stands at the window and stares out at the rocks. At times she thinks she sees a shadow, like a ghost, moving among them. Then, like the fog, the shadow vanishes.

Hannah kneels and stretches out her hand. A half-grown kitten runs toward her, a wisp of a creature with a rusty, raspy purr and eyes as green as the sea itself. She snuggles in Hannah's arms with her head warm and solid beneath Hannah's chin. The kitten is the pale gray of the morning sky before the sun breaks through, and her ears and tail are as dark as night. Her name is Misty.